DATE DUE

MAY 18			
SEP 13			
OCT 13 '80			
NOV 17 '80			
DEC 1 '80			
OC 15 '01			

4277

F
SHU

Shura, Mary Francis
Topcat of Tam   X30050

TOPCAT OF TAM

Mary Francis Shura

TOPCAT OF TAM

illustrated by Charles Robinson

HOLIDAY HOUSE · NEW YORK

*To all lost and frightened little things and their
gentle protectors, this story is dedicated.*

CHAPTER oo ONE

From Timothy's seat he could see right into the school yard. By sitting up very straight he could even see past the school yard into the grove of eucalyptus trees and up the mountainside beyond. He would have been able to see the mountain itself except that almost every day its top was hidden by fingering wisps of pale blue fog.

Mount Tamalpais, with its cap of mystery, was ever so much more interesting to Timothy than anything that went on in Mrs. Janson's fourth grade room.

That cloudy Tuesday morning in October Timothy was, as usual, not paying attention. But he did see everything that happened beyond the window, a towhee hopping along the playground, a lone bee scouting the branches of an acacia bush, and then suddenly, a skinny blue cat coming down the mountain path. The cat walked as if he were the king of the mountain, holding his head as if it supported an invisible crown. He set his feet down a little in front of each other and his tail made a shepherd's crook that swayed gracefully as he walked.

Timothy held his breath with hoping as the cat crossed the school yard (picking his feet up daintily as if he were afraid the cinders might soil them). Then what Timothy hoped for happened. Gathering himself into a great ball of spring, the cat jumped up onto the windowsill right by Timothy. He stood there, looking at Timothy straight on so that their eyes were no farther apart than a ruler.

Because everyone else was paying attention to Mrs. Janson, and because the cat's leap was so spookily silent, nobody saw the cat but Timothy.

Timothy smiled at the cat and slid over in his seat.

The cat cocked his head in a question, then accepted Timothy's invitation. After he pressed warmly against Timothy's side, he curled up and shut his eyes.

Timothy sneaked little looks at the cat. He curved his hand around the cat's warm body feeling the ribs under his fingers. The cat's stomach rose and fell as he breathed.

Timmy pretended he wasn't at school at all. He pretended to be in his own room in the apartment at home. He heard a rap on the door and his teen-age sister Toby peered in.

"May I please, pretty please, come in and pet your cat, Timothy?" she asked in that soft voice she saved to use only when she wanted something.

Timothy yawned and looked at his watch. (He didn't have a watch really, but in daydreams you can have a watch, a huge watch with the day of the week and month on it as well as the hour, one that you could dive under water with and that might even tell you if it was going to rain before you got back home. And it had a red leather band, too.) "For three or four minutes only," he decided aloud. He watched his sister, Toby, walk in respectfully and kneel by the blue cat to pet him.

His little sister Emily would *never never* get to pet the cat. She was a tattle-tale and a spoil-sport and anyway, animals made her sneeze.

Timmy smiled kindly on Toby as she respectfully petted his cat.

"You look very happy, Timothy," Mrs. Janson said suddenly from the front of the room.

"I am," Timothy said honestly enough.

"Would you like to explain to us what there is about our lesson that makes you so happy?" There was just the faintest edge of crossness in her voice, and Timothy was embarrassed.

"I wasn't smiling about the lesson," he admitted. "I was smiling about . . ." then he paused, ". . . something else," he finished quite lamely.

Mrs. Janson was tapping her pointer on her left hand and trying to look pleasant.

"Here it comes . . ." Matthew said half aloud in his flat twangy voice.

"Stand back for a whopper . . ." Johnny added in a laughing whisper.

Timothy flushed so that the red went all the way from his shirt to the edge of his hair. He could hear Jim P. humming. (Jim Prentice was always called Jim P. because there was another Jim in the room called Jim S.) Jim P. was humming that ugly little song that goes "Liar, Liar," etc. "I don't *always* tell stories," Timothy told himself unhappily.

"Children," Mrs. Janson said very firmly, and the voices stopped. "Timothy, I think you might tell us what you are smiling about so that we can all be happy, too."

"No one would believe me anyway," Timothy protested.

"As everyone has told you, Timothy," Mrs. Janson said patiently, "if you just tell the truth, people will believe you."

She was waiting. They were all waiting, smiling that ugly way people do when they think you are going to get into trouble.

"I was watching a blue cat come down from Tamalpais Mountain," Timothy said firmly. Then he just shut his ears to the chorus of jeers that came instantly. The noise was stopped just as instantly at the rap of Mrs. Janson's pointer on the desk.

"A blue cat, Timothy?" Mrs. Janson asked. "And where did the blue cat go?"

"Through the school yard and up on my windowsill."

"Children." Mrs. Janson almost had to shout to be heard. "You will stop those awful noises. And then the blue cat went away so that we could go back to our lesson, isn't that right, Timothy?"

"No Ma'am," Timothy said softly. "He got into my seat with me and is taking a nap."

There was a great clatter as everyone stood up and craned their necks to see Timothy's seat. Mrs. Janson, looking cross at herself for starting the ruckus with her very first question, marched briskly down the aisle toward Timothy's seat.

All the noises, and Timothy's talking and finally the crisp click of Mrs. Janson's shoes had wakened the cat. He yawned and opened his eyes. He stretched one paw lovingly across Timothy's lap and then stood up.

Mrs. Janson's eyes went very wide and her mouth opened without any words coming out at all.

Then, because she was really the nicest fourth grade

teacher anyone ever had (or so Timothy thought), she laughed. She laughed and put her hand on Timothy's shoulder to show that they were friends.

"All of us are sorry for what we thought, Timothy," she said. "For indeed that is a blue cat. In fact, if I remember my cats correctly, that is what is called a Russian Blue cat. Now, how about we put him out the window and go on with our work?"

"Oh, couldn't he stay?" Timothy begged. "He's hungry, you can tell. He's not bothering anyone. And I'll give him some of my lunch . . ."

"Do you think he is a qualified fourth grader?" Mrs. Janson laughed.

"We would all help him to catch up," Diane suggested from the next seat. All the children were clustered around Timothy's seat staring at the cat who studied them wisely with his great golden eyes.

"Oh, please, Mrs. Janson."

"We won't let him distract us."

"Just for today."

"Until we find out whose cat he is."

The chorus of cries was so pleading that Mrs. Janson finally nodded her head.

"But he has to stay at the top of the class," she decided, picking him up gently in her arms.

He purred as she carried him to her desk. "Does someone have a blanket for a blue cat?" she asked, holding him in her arms.

Mindy, in the second seat back, brought her red scarf and laid it carefully in the IN box on Mrs. Janson's desk.

The cat turned around carefully three times, then he curled back to sleep with his long tail draped gracefully across the stack of books beside him.

"If he's at the top of the class, then he's a top cat, isn't he?" Timothy asked as Mrs. Janson turned back to them.

She nodded, smiling. "Until we find out where he really belongs, he is our Topcat."

"But remember," she cautioned, opening her book to begin the work again, "he's Topcat to us, but somewhere, he has a home and people who love him and we will find them, won't we?"

Timothy tried to pretend he hadn't even heard that or he never would have been able to concentrate on his lesson.

When he finally finished his math paper, he began to daydream. He thought of how it would be that night at home. Every night at dinner his family had conversation.

His sister Toby always had stories to tell about what had happened at high school. Mom and Dad listened and asked questions and sometimes laughed very gaily at things she said.

Because his sister Emily was the baby and awfully spoiled, they listened to her carefully too. They laughed because they thought she talked in a cute way.

Tonight he would have a story to tell. And it wouldn't be made up either, as it sometimes had to be. He could tell them about Topcat. Just thinking about how much fun dinner would be made him happy all over.

CHAPTER oo TWO

Fʀᴏᴍ the very first minute that Topcat came, school was thirty million times more fun than before. Take lunch time that first day.

Topcat slept all morning on Mindy's scarf. When the lunch bell clanged, the great noon rustling of lunch sacks began.

Topcat wakened, licked his lips, and leaping gracefully from Mrs. Janson's desk, he walked straight down the aisle to Timothy's seat.

"He's hungry," Timothy said quickly, for fear Mrs. Janson might criticize Topcat for getting up without permission.

"I'm sure he is," Mrs. Janson smiled. "Let me see what I have to share with him."

Everyone fished about in their lunches looking. "Cats are carnivores," Sukie announced seriously, frowning under her dark bangs. "Carnivores eat meat."

"So who doesn't know that," Matthew scoffed. "But I bet he'll like this." He was peeling a hard-boiled egg as he glared at her.

"My mother is a nurse so I know," Sukie said stubbornly. "Cats like mice and moles and birds and fish and . . ."

"Stop her, stop her," Johnny squealed, clutching at his throat.

"Now, Johnny," Mrs. Janson laughed. "You only need to be upset if you happen to have mice and moles in your lunch box."

Mindy, who was always quick to help with anything, brought a big orange napkin from her lunch box for Topcat's plate. The children piled things on it, watching to see what Topcat would eat.

He ate a little piece of the bologna from Timothy's sandwich and would have eaten it all except that Paul put some sliced turkey down beside it. Topcat pretended not to see the eggs or the chips or even the little sausages until the last bite of that turkey was gone.

"Taffy is out with chickenpox so her milk is extra," Kim Wong reminded Mrs. Janson. "Couldn't we just feed it to our cat?"

"That's a very good idea, Kim," Mrs. Janson agreed and poured some of the milk into an art bowl. Topcat lapped it eagerly, his bright tongue lifting a stream of milk into his mouth.

Topcat finished his lunch with a cheese tidbit that Marcia gave him, eating with his head tilted sideways, shaking his head as he chewed the crisp morsel.

"Tomorrow I will bring regular cat food for him," Mrs. Janson told them, as they watched Topcat settle down for a nap in his desk box.

"Tomorrow," Timothy thought happily. "She said tomorrow. That means we can keep him, that he can stay . . ."

"You mean you're going to keep him locked up in the

school room all night," Benny asked, "with no air and no bathroom and no nothing?"

"Of course not," Mrs. Janson said. "We'll leave the window open a crack so he can come in and out. Anyway, he will only stay until we find his owners."

"He doesn't belong to anyone," Timothy said firmly. "He's a mountain cat."

"That's a mountain lion, silly," Matthew said.

"He couldn't have any owners," Kent agreed, "or why would he be so starved looking?"

"He might have strayed away and gotten lost," Mindy suggested in her low soft voice.

"Animals can find their way home from anywhere," Jim S. said. "Mom read a book to me once, about a pet named Shep . . ."

"That was a dog," Paul said disgustedly. "I heard that one too."

"Maybe he was kidnapped from a Russian steamer offshore and smuggled into land and then got away," Timothy suggested. "What if the Russians got afraid of something and pulled anchor and had to go without him no matter what happened . . ."

Groans rose all about him. Timothy sank into his chair.

"That's all the argument we need for *days*," Mrs. Janson said. "We'll run an ad and try to find Topcat's family. Until his owners come, he can live here in our room . . . *if* he doesn't keep people from doing their work."

After a loud chorus of "He won'ts" and "Never" and "Not me," they all went out to play during noon recess.

That night at dinner, Mom served spaghetti and meat

ST. ANDREWS SCHOOL
ROCK FALLS, ILL.

balls. Timothy's big sister told a wonderful story about a basketball game that was being lost very badly. At the last minute her team came rushing in and made a lot of points and won it with everybody cheering.

Timothy's little sister told about falling off the jungle gym at school. She even had a bandage with blue and white stars on it to prove it.

Timothy cleared his throat to make them listen. "Today a blue cat came walking down from the mountain and sat in my seat with me."

Timothy's mother leaned over and tapped his hand. "When are you ever going to learn, Tim?" she said reproachfully.

Timothy started to protest but his father said warningly, "I believe you had better quit when you are ahead, son."

Timothy wouldn't look at his sisters because he didn't want to see the way they were looking back at him. He put a whole meat ball in his mouth at once and it stuck in his throat.

CHAPTER oo THREE

Mrs. Janson brought a copy of the paper with the ad in it. Ann was chosen to read it aloud to the class. Diane put it on the bulletin board with red, white, and blue tape around it.

> FOUND: Russian Blue cat. Full grown. Owner call Mountain View School during hours or Janson, 351–4563 after five.

Timothy couldn't stand to look at that notice. He had thought about Topcat so much since he came. All of Timothy's life he had wanted a pet of his very own, but always there were reasons.

"All kinds of reasons," his mother explained gently. "We aren't allowed to have pets in our apartment, and Emily is allergic to them . . ."

"But we could buy a house," he had protested.

"And get rid of Emily?" his mother laughed. "It isn't that easy. You just cannot have pets, that's all. Worse things have happened to boys."

"I don't believe it," Timothy had told her sullenly.

But now Topcat had come down from the magic mist of

Tamalpais. He had come straight to Timothy as if he were not a regular cat but an answer from all the stars Timothy had ever wished on, or all the white horses he had clapped his fist in his hand for.

Topcat simply must *not* be taken away by any strangers coming in there and claiming him for their own.

Topcat adopted every one of the children as his own. He visited every desk sometime during the day. During roll call and milk money, he played with his Superball. He knocked it wildly all about the room and into people's feet and under their seats. Alison always grinned broadly because she had thought to bring the ball for him.

But Timothy secretly knew that Topcat loved him best and it was Timothy who watched the door for fear of strangers coming.

An older couple, the age of grandparents, came first. The woman was short with crispy gray hair curled all around her face. The gentleman had very pink cheeks. Timothy crossed his fingers as Mrs. Janson invited them in. The lady, whose name was Mrs. Moore, had on knee pants above very skinny legs that ended in great white tennis shoes. She knelt down by Topcat and looked at him a long time, stroking him and examining him carefully.

Then she stood up again with a little "oof." She asked sharply, "What is your opinion, Herbert?"

Mr. Moore, who hadn't said a word until then, shook his head from side to side. "That is not Myron," he said with certainty.

"But are you sure?" she asked crossly. "You have to be *sure*."

"His face is too broad. His tail not nearly long enough," Mr. Moore said very firmly.

Timothy wanted to leap to his feet and argue. Topcat's face was perfect. His tail was beautiful. Then Timothy remembered that if Mr. Moore had said "yes," Topcat would have gone away with them.

The whole class slumped with relief when the Moores left.

Timothy was even more scared when a dapper young man parked his sports car by the school yard where Timothy could see him. Tim's heart sank as the man walked briskly down the walk to the school, carrying a leather pouch with lots of straps.

Timothy just knew this man would march in and march right out again with Topcat inside that big leather pouch.

Sure enough, the man did come to the room.

Sure enough, he studied Topcat seriously, looking at him this way and that. Then he asked how the cat came to be there and a lot of other questions. The bag held a camera and lights and he took lots of pictures of Topcat.

Then he thanked them very nicely for their time and said he had really come because he had never seen a Russian Blue and was curious. "I am a reporter and I thought there might be a story in this," he explained.

Everyone smiled at him when he left, nodding at them smartly from the door.

Every day Topcat seemed more at home. And every day someone thought of a new toy to amuse him.

Johnny brought a huge shoe of his father's. Topcat loved to crawl into the shoe reaching with his paw for what might

hide in the toe. Sometimes he took the shoe-lace in his mouth and dragged the shoe along after him, letting it bump noisily.

On Friday morning, Kelly raised the question first.

"What will happen to Topcat over the weekend?"

Mrs. Janson tapped her pencil on her finger and frowned. "Does anyone have any ideas?"

Lots of hands went up at once, pumping the air of the room.

Even Topcat stopped rolling his ball to stare at the forest of hands.

"Paul," Mrs. Janson said, "what is your idea?"

"I don't have any big dogs. I could take him home," he said eagerly.

"Me too," "I want him." The whole room was a chorus of cries until Mrs. Janson clapped her hands over her ears and said, "Cease, desist. Silence."

"Everybody wants to take him home. But I found him first," Timothy grumbled as the noise died down.

"We could have a lottery, and draw names," Kent said. "That would be fair."

There was a murmur of agreement and Mrs. Janson asked, "What do you think of Kent's idea. Would that be fair?"

"Would everybody get a turn?" Kelly asked. "It won't be fair unless everybody gets a turn."

"We can't tell," Mrs. Janson said, "but we could draw names for all the weekends. If Topcat's owner comes, those later people wouldn't have their turn. But if no owner comes, then everyone would have a turn."

"That sounds fair." "That's okay." "Let's draw names,"

came Kent's and Sukie's and Karen's voices all at once,

Mrs. Janson talked very seriously to them while they were writing their names on the pieces of yellow paper.

"There is just one thing," she said carefully. "If you have a reason why you can't take Topcat home, if your parents don't like animals, or it wouldn't be safe to have a cat visitor, don't put your name in at all. Only the people who *really* can have a cat for a weekend guest should put their names in."

Timothy watched the others, almost holding his breath.

Susie had already written her name. She tore it up sadly.

"My dog Stach hates cats," she said quietly. "I don't think I could keep him safe."

"I have to spend weekends with my daddy in Oakland," Tony said, crumpling his paper in his hand with a frown.

Two or three other children tore up their names. Timothy watched them, feeling very guilty. There had to be some way for him to take Topcat home. Surely he could think of a way. He lettered his name carefully telling himself all the time that he would think of a way before his turn really came.

Since Susie and Tony didn't have their names in the box Susie shook the names up and held the box while Tony drew the slips out and read them aloud.

There wasn't a sound in the room as Tony unfolded the first paper. "Benny," he read firmly.

Benny leaped straight up in his chair with a whoop, then came down hard with a giggle.

"Benny . . . October 17 and 18," Mrs. Janson said, writing it on the calendar by the blackboard.

"Alison . . . October 23 to 24," she wrote down as Tony pulled the next slip.

"Katie, October 30, November 1."

"That's Hallowe'en," Jim S. said suddenly. "You get the cat on Hallowe'en!"

Alison giggled. "I could be a witch this year with my very own cat."

"You could be Baba Yaga," Sonya said softly, her dark eyes gleaming. "Baba Yaga is a Russian witch with a chicken-leg house and very much magic!"

"Baba Yaga," some of the children squealed.

Timothy listened, barely breathing as the names went on and on. Was his name never going to be called?

"Timothy . . ." Mrs. Janson grinned at him as she wrote it down.

"February 13. Why, that's a holiday weekend too! You will have three days because of Lincoln's birthday."

"Three days," someone said enviously. Timothy sat very still holding the three days tight in his mind, wondering how he could manage to have Topcat and keep him. Could he talk his mother into letting him have Topcat for three whole days?

That afternoon, Mrs. Janson decorated an orange box and stapled a sturdy muslin handle to both ends of the box. Top-cat, skittering around and looking a little wild-eyed, went home with Benny for the first of his weekend visits.

That night at dinner, Mom served wieners on buns with baked beans, Timothy's big sister Toby told about a musician from India who had come to assembly. He played an instrument called a sitar. Timothy's little sister Emily told about how Ron, the boy in the seat next to hers, had started to get red spots in the middle of recess and the school nurse sent him home.

Timothy announced, "In our room, we are going to get to check out our blue cat like a library book."

Everybody laughed except Toby, who said, "I don't think his silly lies are funny."

"He'll learn," Dad said comfortably. "Just don't bring home any cats that won't fit on the bookshelf." Then Dad had a story of his own to tell and Timothy had lost his turn and nobody believed him again.

CHAPTER oo FOUR

THE weeks sped by quickly. For a long time no one had come to inquire about the ad and Mrs. Janson stopped running it in the paper. Timothy became hopeful that the cat might be theirs forever.

Alison's mother made her a witch's dress for Hallowe'en. She looked terrible with a scraggly wig and a ragged broom in her hand. Timothy was a ghost with one huge green eye where his face should have been. His sister Toby painted it on with marking pencils. She also lent him green knee socks to wear over his feet and hands so he would look even scarier.

That Friday the children pasted cut-out bats and a huge pumpkin face on the box that Alison carried Topcat home in. And Timothy was one week closer to his own turn.

The castle they made for Topcat's Christmas present was Tony's idea. Everybody brought something to make it beautiful. Billy's father dropped off a huge stack of cardboard boxes from the grocery store where he worked. Katie and Paul brought silver paint. Marcia and Sukie made the banners that flew from the high turrets with iron-on tape. When it was all through, Timothy only had to narrow his

eyes a little bit and the castle looked as real as the ones in the fairy tale books.

The day of the Christmas party they let down the drawbridge and invited Topcat in.

At first he was wary of it, walking about the moat and switching his tail as if to warn the castle to behave. Finally his curiosity won. He walked over the drawbridge and peered into the great kingly hall with its nice soft rug made of a woolly orange towel.

He stayed in there a long time. Once in a while Timothy could see his eyes peer from a turret window or see a banner shake as he made a grand tour.

Then Topcat came to the great front door and lay down with his head on the drawbridge and went to sleep guarding his castle.

Mrs. Janson took Topcat home for Christmas. She said it wouldn't be fair for any one child to have him for two whole weeks like that.

In January the magic mists that clouded the head of Mount Tamalpais grew thicker and whiter. Timothy watched the clouds as the class studied about the Indians who once lived there. Timothy understood why the Miwoks themselves feared the top of the great mountain. Something hidden and mystical stirred in that mist. Timothy was sure that Topcat had come from that mist-draped world, that he was really a magic cat from the high meadows of Tam. For if he were not magic, how could one cat be so wise and so tender all at once like the spirit of the gentle natives of that misty mountain?

Then it was February, the fifth of February, and in only

one more week Topcat would come home with Timothy. Mom served meat loaf that night at dinner, with little brown vegetables cooked all around it in the pan.

Timothy crossed his fingers under the table while his father carefully sliced the steaming loaf.

He watched his father put two potatoes, one carrot and a tiny round brown onion on his plate. Timothy didn't like cooked carrots and he couldn't stand onions fixed any way at all but he didn't say a word.

His sister Toby was talking. She told about how a friend of hers had had a skiing accident up in Squaw Valley and how the whole art class had made designs on her cast.

His little sister Emily said that her teacher had brought a great big box of paper lace and red paper and shiny small flowers and they were going to make their very own designs for Valentine's cards.

"All the kids are getting to check out Topcat for weekends," Timothy said quickly, between bites, to get his turn.

"Topcat?" his mother inquired.

"The blue cat," Toby said sarcastically. "The one who is checked out like a library book and lives in a castle with a moat."

"Come on, Toby," Timothy pleaded. "He's real."

"I'm allergic to real cats," Emily said smugly, as if it were something to be proud of.

"Oh," Mother nodded vaguely, "that one. You are not eating your vegetables, Timmy."

Timothy took a bite of carrot and placed it carefully on the back of his tongue so he could swallow it down without tasting it.

"Kim Wong lives in an apartment like we do and she took Topcat home last week," Timothy said.

"Her apartment must have different rules than ours," Dad commented.

"Or maybe they just especially let her . . . just for one weekend like that," Timothy suggested.

Timothy's mother was frowning a little, staring at him.

"Are you trying to ask us something, son?" she said.

"I sure would love to have my turn at having Topcat visit," he said, the quick band of hope stretching tight inside his chest.

"Timmy," his mother said gently, "If there *is* such a cat, and if he is being checked out as you say, I am sorry we didn't believe you before. But in any case, it simply isn't possible for us to have a cat here."

"Not even just for a weekend?" Timothy pleaded.

Dad shook his head. "It's just not possible. You know what an old dragon Mrs. Nelson is!"

"John!" Timothy's mother rebuked his father firmly. Mrs. Nelson was their landlady. Every time Dad called her a dragon, Timothy's mother gave the same word-for-word lecture to him. "You mustn't say things like that about Mrs. Nelson. She is only doing her job."

"Looking fierce and breathing fire are not in anyone's job description," Dad said mildly, serving himself some more salad.

Mom only frowned that time. "Your father is right, Timothy. It isn't possible for you to bring a cat here."

Emily looked up smugly and said, "Cats make me sneeze."

"Oh, you," Timothy said angrily. "Even if I kept him in

my room, and kept Spoil-sport Emily out and took him for walks when Mrs. Nelson was away and everything?"

"Don't you think that would be sneaking?" Dad asked.

Timothy dropped his eyes from his father's direct gaze. "You just don't understand how much I *want* him," he said quietly. But Timothy knew there was nothing more he could say to his father right then. He would simply have to think of a way. And there wasn't much time left.

For the next few days Timothy forgot to smile or laugh or even answer questions. He was thinking. But no matter what stories he made up and told himself, no matter how much he blamed his problem on other people (like Mrs. Nelson), the problem remained the same . . . there were only two choices, like heads or tails on a nickel.

On Wednesday night the moon was full. Timothy lay across his bed staring at the full moon of February. He thought of how the Indians called it the hunger moon because it was the month of the year with no harvest. The seeds had been gathered and ground into meal. The last of the acorns were being made into cakes. The hunting was slim and the salmon were not running the rivers.

The moon lit the crown of mist on Tamalpais. Topcat had come from there to him, not to anyone else.

In the band of moonlight streaming across his bed, Timothy pried the back off his coin bank. He tossed a nickel high and slapped it on the back of his hand as he had seen the big guys do.

"Tails, I tell them I can't take him. Heads, I hide him here."

He lifted his hand and the Indian head stared at him. He

put the coin back into his bank and started making his plans.

First he needed a place to hide his cat.

There was lots of space in the laundry room but Mrs. Nelson and Mom were both down there every day.

The only space in his own room was under the bed and what cat would scrounch down there for three days?

In his mind he checked the furnace room, and the locker storage room. There was simply no place at all.

Then Timothy thought of the great Monterey pine beyond the alley outside his bedroom window. It was the largest tree around anywhere and a favorite place for nesting birds. Deep in its green prickles were great hiding limbs with climbing steps along the trunk. Loud Pacific Jays bounced from limb to limb, scolding. Sometimes in the night Timothy heard the hollow questioning of an owl from its depths.

He knew a special branch, half way up. He could fasten Topcat's box there, making sure the air holes were open.

He could take food to Topcat there, and water.

Then he could take Topcat up to the mountain meadows to play where no one could see.

Even as Timothy watched, the moon disappeared into the mists that crowned Mount Tam. It would go down behind that mountain and into the sea crashing on the cliff beyond.

A night bird wailed sadly from somewhere in the dark.

"Topcat will like that," Timothy decided. "That's just what Topcat would really like the most, a weekend in a tree." Tomorrow Topcat was coming home with him—the very next day.

CHAPTER oo FIVE

THE day that was marked "TIMOTHY" on the calendar came all in scarlet and gray. The sky and the fingering mists and the steady dropping of rain were all gray. Sidewalks, streets, and a heavy bank of clouds in the east were an even deeper gray.

But Mrs. Janson's room was strung with scarlet hearts and flowery roses and all the brightness of Valentine's Day.

Timothy plodded off to school bundled against the rain from boots through cap. His stomach was tight with how the day would end. All day he watched Topcat doze on the drawbridge of his castle. Then the last bell rang and he packed Topcat into his carrying case to start home.

The rain was messing up his carefully made plans. He couldn't take his coat off and drape it over the box on the way home as he had planned. Instead he plodded along with the Valentine-covered box right out there for anyone to see —including Mom, if she should happen to look out the window.

Timothy turned the corner a block before reaching his own apartment house and cut back through the alley to reach the big tree.

There were only bedroom windows like his own facing on the alley. Timothy watched the windows carefully as he passed, hoping that no one would happen to be looking out.

Climbing the tree with Topcat's box was not as easy as Timothy had thought. The slightest touch against a branch and great showers of droplets fell on him. His foot kept slipping on the wet limbs and he had to set the box down carefully each time he climbed even one limb.

Finally he reached the right branch. Using the rope he had kept in his coat pocket all day, he tied Topcat's box securely into the crotch of the tree.

He was halfway down when suddenly he felt so sad he had to stop. Looking back up he could see one of Topcat's golden eyes gazing at him through a tiny air hole.

He climbed back up and took Topcat out. The big cat purred and rubbed against him as they sat there on the limb. Timothy explained to Topcat over and over as he put him back into the box before clambering down the tree.

Timothy's mother waved silently at him as he came in. She was on the phone and was nodding to the other person seriously and now and then saying a quick word.

Timothy walked past Emily and her small doll to look into the refrigerator.

"Hi, sweetheart," his mother called after the phone clicked. "Miserable day. Hungry?"

"Not really," he admitted, holding still while she kissed him on the top of his head. "We had Valentine cookies and punch in a cup."

"Of course, that's right," she said. "Glass of milk?"

He nodded and she filled his blue mug.

Timothy drank his milk standing up. Then he went to his own room. He stared through his window into the tree trying to see Topcat's box. Of course it was hidden among the limbs.

He felt restless and funny. He didn't want to play anything or talk to anyone. All he wanted to do was go out and see if Topcat was all right.

He had started out the door when he heard his mother's surprised call.

"Yes Ma'am?" he replied not really going back in.

"Isn't it raining?"

"Not any more," he assured her, "and I have my rain stuff on."

"Well, don't get wet, and don't stay out long."

Timothy grinned at her. "I can have fun can't I?"

She made a face and said, "Oh, go bike."

He was halfway down the walk on his bike when she called after him, "Come back if one drop falls, okay?"

"Okay," he called and pedaled away fast before she changed her mind.

First he wheeled all around the block avoiding the alley. Then he wheeled around the block again before going down the alley to where the tree was. He looked around carefully before leaning his bike on the grass and starting up the tree.

He had Topcat out of the box and was holding him in his arms when he heard a voice call.

"You up there, boy?"

He scrambled Topcat into the box and peered down through the branches.

Mrs. Nelson's face was staring up at him angrily.

"Yes, Mrs. Nelson," he said, his throat hurting with being scared.

"What are you doing up there in my tree?"

"I just like to climb trees," he said, starting to climb down. It wasn't that he thought she could possibly climb up after him but he was so scared that he clambered down the tree. His feet scraped on branches and there was a great crackling of a limb that he stepped on too far out. His face flamed from the scratch of prickly needles as he dropped on the grass beside her.

She stood glaring at him, shaking her head. "If I live to a hundred," she said, "I'll never understand boys. What's so big about scratching yourself up and getting all pine-sticky in a tree?"

Her hands were on her hips and her head was thrust forward at him. Her words came so fast and so hotly that Timothy thought of a dragon just as his father had said.

"And what's more to the point, young man," she shouted, seeming to get madder as she went along, "it takes more than your lifetime and mine to grow a tree that tall in these parts. Worth hundreds of dollars, they are, trees like that. You just keep your feet out of my trees or I'll have to have a talk with your mom. Do you understand me?" Her tone was very threatening. Timothy nodded vigorously.

"Yes, Mrs. Nelson, I do, Mrs. Nelson, I won't, Mrs. Nelson, I'm sorry, Mrs. Nelson."

He kept looking at her and nodding until he got to his bike and got on.

"I am sorry, Mrs. Nelson," he said again and she seemed to relax a little.

"You just remember," she shouted after him, still standing there.

He wanted her to go away. What if Topcat cried in the tree or howled, or the box (which he had left untied) fell off the limb?

He rode off slowly on his bike. Finally at the corner he saw her turn and go back into the apartment house.

He heaved a huge sigh of relief.

Later that evening he crept out and tied the box securely. He fed Topcat some cat food and gave him some water he had brought in a little jar.

The wind rose with evening. Even though there was no new rain, the gusts of wind swept great splashes from the trees that washed against the windows. The darkness of the starless night hid even the shape of the mountain from view.

It took Timothy a long time to go to sleep. Having Topcat for himself was so different from how he had dreamed it would be. He felt sadder than he could ever remember. Every time the wind howled he thought he heard, mixed in with it, the lonely cry of his friend in the box high in the Monterey pine.

CHAPTER oo SIX

Tᴉᴍᴏᴛʜʏ wakened with a start. The howl of the wind had ceased. He ran to the window and looked out into the big tree. Every needle glistened with droplets of rain but the air was still. In the empty alley, the weeds were bowed by rain. The puddles looked desolate and lonely.

More than anything Timothy wanted to go out to check on Topcat. Instead he dressed hastily and went to the kitchen. Emily was already glued to the Saturday cartoons on TV. His mother smiled at him sleepily from the stove.

"I heard you stirring about," she smiled. "Pancakes in two minutes."

When he had finished eating he excused himself and started for the coat closet.

"You don't want to go out?" his mother asked with amazement. "It's drowned out there! Wait until the sun dries things off."

"I like it this way," Timothy pleaded.

She hesitated, then grinned. "All right, but boots. Big plans for today?"

Timothy's heart thumped. All his life he had made up stories to tell. All his life people had called them fibs or lies. Now he was really lying and he didn't feel the same at all. Something hurt inside and kept him from being able to look at his mother straight.

"Billy and I," he said uneasily. "In fact, I might even stay all day, lunch and all."

"Are you sure that's all right with his mom?" she asked, a little worried.

"He asked me," Timothy lied. If his mother let him go, he could take Topcat far away, up into the meadows and they could play together all day.

"Okay. Just stay dry, honey," she cautioned.

Timothy decided against his bike. The bike had given him away with Mrs. Nelson the time before. He walked to the end of the block whistling, then turned the corner. The alley was empty. He tiptoed along carefully. People might be getting up. He didn't want them looking out at him.

At the tree he looked all around again. He had not *prom-ised* Mrs. Nelson anything, but he didn't want her "having a talk" with Mom about him.

He was only two limbs up the tree when he saw it. He clung to the tree and almost cried out. The orange box with its lid only half on, all out of shape and darkened by rain, was hanging at a tilt against the tree trunk.

When he scrambled to it, he found the cans of food and the little coffee can of kibbles still in the corner. But Top-cat was gone.

Timothy sat on the branch a long time feeling shocked and very, very unhappy.

What could he do? He could never go back to school without Topcat. He could never tell Mom and Dad what he had done, even if they could help.

He would have to look for Topcat until he found him. If he didn't find him . . . Timothy couldn't stand to think of that. He let himself down slowly from the tree and stood there a long minute looking around.

Where would a scared wet kitty go in the middle of the night in a storm?

He walked back into the field behind the apartment house. The weeds were high and thick and bowed with moisture.

"Kitty," he called softly. "Here kitty, kitty. Topcat."

There was no answer, only the chirping of birds clustered in the trees that marched up the road toward Mount Tamalpais.

Timothy walked all the streets near his house. He even walked over to school and back, looking at the window of Mrs. Janson's room where Topcat had come first.

There was no sign of the cat anywhere.

He wanted to cry. It was so hopeless. How could he ever ever figure out where Topcat had gone?

He walked past the school to a street he never played on.

An old man with a wide-toothed rake was sweeping soggy fallen leaves from his walk. His face was brown and lined and he wore a faded blue hat pushed back from bushy eyebrows. He stopped and looked at Timothy as he passed.

"Morning, son," he said without smiling.

"Morning," Timothy said, not even trying to smile.

"You don't seem so bright this nice morning," the old man said thoughtfully.

"I've lost my cat," Timothy said. "You haven't seen a cat around here this morning have you?"

The old man cocked his head and frowned.

"Matter of fact, no," he said. "Not that I really know of. But the dogs were chasing some animal this morning before I was out. I thought it might be a 'coon because it took off up the hill." He pointed his rake toward the road that led up to the high meadows of Tamalpais. "I figured only a varmint would aim for such a wild place."

"Then did the dogs come back?" Timothy asked, breathless with hope.

"So they did, after a bit. But I don't know if it was a cat," he reminded Timothy.

"Thanks a lot sir," Timothy said, starting off at a run. "I'll take the chance."

There were several more blocks with sidewalk as the road went up the hill. Then the sidewalks disappeared. There was only the wet curved bed of the road lined by trees with an occasional driveway down to where houses clung to the hillside overlooking the valley he was leaving.

Before long Timothy took off his ski jacket. Walking the hill was moist hot work. Every time he stopped to rest he would call Topcat. Sometimes a faint echo would answer, springing back from the curve of a valley. Once he flushed a doe and a fawn who crashed off in great triangles through the buck brush and wild licorice and disappeared among the trees.

Timothy had never walked this far up the mountain alone before. He knew the mountain farther up, because Mom and Dad took them in the car to picnics there. But he had never walked the wet fragrance of the woods. He took shortcuts and went from one loop of the road to another, but his

heart was sinking. The mountain was huge and high. It seemed to go on forever before it plunged down again to the beaches at Stinson and Bolinas and the crashing sea.

People passed along the road. There were cars full of families in station wagons with picnic baskets in the back. Timothy was getting hungry. The thought of the full picnic baskets made his mouth water.

Every once in a while he got scared and discouraged. He thought of going back and telling the kids he had lost Topcat. Since he couldn't do that, he kept on walking and calling. There was a chance, just a tiny hope of a chance that Topcat would hear him.

He stopped and watched a group of cyclists go by in the road. There were three of them, two boys and a girl. They were riding ten-speed bikes, and were bent like bows over the handle bars. None of them even looked up. They rode on like curved singing ghosts.

The sun was high overhead when Timothy reached the last of the heavily wooded mountainside and came upon the high meadows of Tam. Red-tailed hawks swung in lazy circles and floated on the updrafts from the mountain.

Then Timothy heard a distant sound. Far below him along the pale sickle of sand the surf was pounding on the beach below. The blue of the sea was blinding.

Away out to sea Timothy saw a cluster of fishing boats spaced along the horizon.

He was so awfully tired, and the sun on the hill was growing warm. He slumped into the grass and curled up, his folded ski jacket under his head.

"When I am rested," he told himself drowsily, "I will find Topcat, right here on his mountain."

CHAPTER oo SEVEN

Wʜᴇɴ Timothy wakened, the sun had crossed over his head and was sinking towards the far line of the sea. From below he could hear the surf crashing in great roars against the base of the cliff. Lower than the golden sun, along the line of water, a deep mist rolled toward the land like an immense white blanket being unfolded by invisible hands.

Even as he watched, the shoreline disappeared and the mist began to rise through the ravines. With the mist a silence came. The birds about him grew still. Even the high swinging hawks veered away from the strands of fog as if the mist were a separate wall dividing the mountain from the rest of the world.

Timothy thought of the legends of the mountain, of how the Indians who called it their home never ventured to the top for fear of the spirit that lived in the high mist.

He thought of running, of fleeing faster than the mist. Maybe he could be on the other side of the mountain before it reached him.

He turned and started to run. His stomach ached from fear and hunger. He ran awkwardly, stumbling through the meadow strewn with great rocks. All about him gleamed the golden heads of small poppies.

But he did not stop to look at anything. The chill of the mist was suddenly upon him and all about him. He veered to the right to avoid a great rocky outcrop studded with trees. He missed his footing and fell on into the thick grass that smelled spicy from some wild herb among the grasses.

He rubbed his hurt ankle a minute. Then he got to his feet slowly, trying his weight on the foot. It hurt but he could still walk.

As he took the first painful step he thought he heard something in the mist. He stared all about him. The gnarled trees in among the giant rocks were now almost hidden by mist. Then his eyes played a strange trick on him. He thought he saw something move among the trees. Timothy stood very still, numb with terror, as one of the trees moved slowly from among the others and started across the meadow toward him.

The whimsy of the wind stirred the mist and Timothy cried out in relief. The moving figure was not a tree at all but a man. He carried a pack high on his shoulders and in his hand he held a gnarled walking cane. His thick beard was shaped like a spade except that it grew wispy at the ends so that it blew about his face. His jacket was loose, of stained leather with fringes all about like Buffalo Bill's.

As the man came nearer, Timothy drew back from him. His eyes were remarkably blue and solemn—even threatening.

"Why are you pulling away?" the man asked, his low voice muted by the wind. "Are you afraid?"

"A little," Timothy admitted.

"Of me?" the man asked without a change of expression.

"Yes, sir," Timothy said. "I thought you were . . ."

"The spirit of this place," the man suggested as Timothy faltered.

"No sir, I thought you were a tree."

Timothy imagined that under his beard the man almost smiled. "Sometimes I am a tree," the man replied dreamily. "Sometimes a great stone. Sometimes I am even a gull wheeling wide circles over the hills."

Timothy listened without moving.

"But I am always the spirit of this mountain, and you have no business here at nightfall, a child like you."

"But I do have business," Timothy said, reaching down to rub his aching ankle. "I am looking for my cat."

"Your cat?" the man asked.

"Well, partly my cat," Timothy corrected himself.

"Why should the cat be here?"

"He came from here, from the mountain, in the first place," Timothy said, "and when he got away . . ."

"Got away," the man repeated somberly. "Then he was a prisoner?"

"Not a prisoner," Timothy said, very unhappy now. The man didn't seem to understand anything he said. "He was living in a tree . . . with me."

"You do not look like a boy who lives in a tree," the man said reproachfully. "And if the cat came from this place and chose to return, you have no right to force him back to you."

"But, sir . . ."

The man shook his head reproachfully. "The mists of this mountain should be left in peace. All creatures who fear im-

prisonment are in this mist, owls and hawks, small hares and the sleepy-eyed vultures. Perhaps your cat is here too, but you could never find him. The mist hides all of us who flee from streets and houses."

"But sir, I can't . . . go . . ."

"You must," the man said. "You are not safe here."

The last faint line of scarlet light died along the edge of the sea.

"Already Japan is turning to gold," the man said, following Timothy's eyes. "All of Tamalpais will sink into blackness, and its own mist. Go."

Timothy was so tired and so hungry, his ankle ached so badly that he began to cry.

"I don't know the way," he sobbed. "I am lost. I really am."

"Where do you live?" the man asked. As Timothy hesitated, the man spoke roughly . . . "Stinson? Bolinas? Sausalito? San Francisco? Mill Valley? San Rafael?"

As Timothy nodded, the man started to walk.

The man led him across the meadow and through some trees where they came upon a trail.

"Follow this," the man said. "After a few yards it will come to a paved road. Follow that road straight all the way down. It will lead you home."

"Thank you, sir," Timothy said. He started walking slowly.

Timothy walked obediently for a while, then he looked back. The man was gone.

Timothy sat down on a rock to think.

The silence that had come with the mist was going away.

It was as if the day had been put to sleep and the night was now waking. Timothy listened to the scritch of some creature in the underbrush, he heard the long low cry of a bird from the hill beyond and the hollow cry of an owl.

He knew he should go on down the mountain to home. But if he went without Topcat, he need not go at all.

There was no sound of the man's footfall. Maybe he really was the spirit of the mountain. Timothy shrugged. If he was, and if he was right about the mist, then Timothy would have to seek Topcat back up there in the mist himself, no matter how scary it was.

CHAPTER oo EIGHT

Tɪᴍᴏᴛʜʏ silently left the path and started back the way he had just come. He remembered what the book about Indians had said. When Indians walked in the valley, they followed the stream bed. When they walked in the mountains they walked two rods below the crest of a hill. He would circle that place where he had met the spirit of the mountain. He would go back into the mist and find Topcat even if the search took him to meadows he didn't know.

Timothy guessed what two rods would be and walked along the ridge. The mist grew steadily colder. Even with his ski parka on, he felt wet clear to the skin.

He practiced pretending to be brave to keep from crying out when wide-winged birds rose suddenly from hiding near his path. They beat the air with a swishing thunder as they rose.

He was sure that he had gone well past the place where the man had been before he started calling again, "Kitty, here kitty. Topcat."

He could feel someone listening but there was no answer. From the mist small eyes glinted greenly from trees and shrubs. Sometimes the path was open and grassy, sometimes

Timothy stumbled through thorny brush and past great stones. Somewhere in the mist he must find Topcat.

Suddenly the voice of the sea rose toward Timothy as if it were calling from a deep well. Timothy stopped and looked about with confusion. He must have reached the edge of one of those high cliffs whose sheer sides reached up many hundreds of feet straight from the sands of the beach. The jagged edge of the cliff could be very near but the thick mist cut off his vision right before his face.

But he could not stand there forever! He slid a foot forward carefully, feeling for footing.

He drew courage from the firmness under his step and slid a foot forward again. This time the earth gave way beneath his weight and he slipped. He grabbed the air desperately and caught the prickly branch of a bush. He clung to it with all his might. He heard far below him at the base of the cliff the thunder of the sea and an avalanche of rocks tumbling down the cliff's side, crashing and pounding with the rattling rhythm of loose earth following. The bush he was clinging to was losing its grip on the cliff. Timothy felt about desperately for a foothold but there was none. With a strange little squeak, the bush, strained by Timothy's weight, pulled loose from its niche. Timothy, the prickly bush still in his aching hand, plunged down the cliff's side towards whatever lay hidden in the mist below.

Timothy remembered calling out. He remembered a sharp pain in his shoulder as he fell against the hill, but he didn't remember landing. The mist just turned to blackness. There was nothing left at all.

Suddenly the blackness blazed into a circle of blinding

light like a cold sun very near his face. Voices were shouting and he heard the hum of a motor very near.

"Easy now," a man's voice spoke very near his ear. "Watch that leg."

Timothy struggled to rise but was held down. "Wait a bit, sport," the voice cautioned. "We'll get you out." Although the mist was dense, the orb of the searchlight was stronger. Timothy realized he was lying on the edge of the mountain road. The searchlight was from the State patrol car behind him. Two crisply uniformed officers were rapidly shovelling him out. He was half buried by stones and dirt he had dislodged in his fall down the side of the cliff.

When Timothy tried to stand up, he discovered that the ankle he had hurt earlier was too swollen now to bear his weight, and his shoulder ached painfully from his fall.

One of the State troopers shone his light up the side of the cliff. Timothy stared at the ragged height of the cliff's face and saw the jagged steepness of the place where he had fallen. Timothy could almost feel his heart tighten with fear at the sight.

"You're lucky to be breathing, son," the officer said, "after that fall."

Then suddenly he sounded cross. "What were you doing up there at night anyway? Who are you? Where are your folks?"

Timothy wanted to answer but he couldn't make the words come.

"Give the kid a chance," the other patrolman said gently. "One question at a time. Can you walk, son?"

Timothy tried, and with help, limped over to the car.

One of the State troopers, the one with the broad face and the gentle voice, began to ask questions slowly. "First tell us who you are."

When Timothy gave his name and address, the patrolmen nodded at each other. "Had a 'missing boy' report on you this evening. You had your folks pretty scared. Did you get lost on the mountain?"

"No sir," Timothy replied. "My cat was lost."

"But you weren't," the man laughed. "Clear across Mount Tam from home but you weren't lost!"

While he talked on the short wave radio, Timothy watched the other State trooper place warning flares around the rock fall on the road. Then he slowly drove along the winding mountain road toward home.

"Tell us again why you were on the mountain alone at that time of night," the trooper asked him after a while.

Timothy wanted to explain it clearly but he was so tired, and he was hungry and his head hurt. "I lost a cat that belonged to all of us," he said tiredly, "and I couldn't go back without him. Then I met the spirit of the mountain . . ."

"Now just a minute," the officer said. "Who was this you met?"

"He said he was the spirit of the mountain," Timothy said. "That's all the name he gave me. That sometimes he was a rock and sometimes a tree and sometimes . . ."

"I think you've had a real bump on the head, Timothy," the officer said. "Why don't you just not try to talk until we get you home?"

CHAPTER oo NINE

THAT night and the next day blurred together in Timothy's mind like a long bad dream. His mother had a red-eyed look that showed she had been crying a lot and seeing her that way made Timothy feel guilty and unhappy.

Dr. Lang checked him all over, making funny clucking noises and frowning at Timothy's shoulder and ankle. The taped bandages that the doctor put on the ankle and shoulder weren't so bad, but Timothy really had to grit his teeth when Dr. Lang treated the scratches with a strong-smelling sticky stuff on a cotton swab.

Timothy dozed and wakened and dozed again until time lost any sense for him. Sometimes his mother was there when he wakened and sometimes it was his big sister Toby smiling very sweetly and being nicer to him than he could ever remember.

At one point he wakened to find a man there with his mother.

"Timothy," his mother called softly when she saw his eyes open. "You remember Mr. Hardesty, don't you? He's a reporter from the paper. He came to see your cat at school a long time ago."

"Hi, Timothy," the man said, smiling cordially. Timothy recognized him at once as the dapper young man who had come to his classroom.

"Hi yourself," Timothy said, hitching himself up on the pillows his mother handed him. "Sure I remember. You have that same leather case."

"My camera," Mr. Hardesty explained. "I'd like to talk about your adventure up on Tam."

"How did you find out about it?" Timothy asked curiously.

"Easy," Mr. Hardesty grinned. "I listen in on police calls all the time on my short wave. When I heard the State patrol call the Sheriff's office to report you were found, I got right on it. That's a reporter's job, you know."

Mr. Hardesty was easy to talk to, maybe too easy, Timothy decided later. Timothy told him the whole story, all about how he couldn't have pets, clear through the man on the mountain and what he looked like and what he said.

Timothy felt great while Mr. Hardesty was there. He could see Toby and Emily lurking just outside the door watching and listening. It made him feel like someone really important to have a strange man listening like that, really listening to what he said and believing him.

But after Mr. Hardesty left, Timothy slept again and forgot all about the interview until his father brought the paper in to show him.

Timothy stared at the front page with disbelief.

In the first place, he looked about six years old in that photo, taken all propped up on the pillows in his striped pajamas. In the second place, now everyone in the whole world knew that he had lost Topcat. And worst of all, when Mr. Hardesty quoted Timothy about meeting the spirit of the mountain, it made Timothy sound like the awfullest crazy liar in fifty states.

"I won't ever go to school again," Timothy announced to his father, putting the paper face down so he wouldn't have to see that silly picture.

"Now come on," his father grinned. "Of course you will."

"Not so long as I live," Timothy promised crossly. "In fact, I may never put my clothes on or leave my room again."

His mother came in, bringing him another glass of chocolate milk. "Of course you will," she said genially. "Dr. Lang says you can make it by the first bell Monday. Don't be such a goose. Everybody makes mistakes."

Sunday came and Timothy felt so much better that he really wanted to get up and out of his room. He ate everything on his breakfast tray and sent Emily back for seconds of cinnamon toast.

"But I still don't feel good enough to go back to school tomorrow," he told his father defensively.

"Too bad about that," his father said with that friendly firmness that Timothy knew he couldn't fight, " 'cause you are going to go anyway."

When Timothy's mother called him Monday morning he woke with a groan.

"Up. Up. Up." she called brightly, the second time she passed his door.

Timothy sat on the side of his bed, rubbing his sore shoulder gingerly and feeling sorry for himself.

"Want some help dressing?" his mother asked pointedly, sticking her head in again.

After breakfast, Timothy tried again. "Do I *have* to go really, Dad," he pleaded. "With my sore ankle and everything?"

"If I have to walk you by the back of the collar like a marionette with no strings," his father replied, smiling but firm.

So Timothy, still limping from his sore ankle, started out for school. He didn't even look up, for fear he'd see some neighbor grinning at him in a funny way with the sides of his mouth which meant "here comes that sappy kid."

At the corner, he heard someone call. Because it wasn't a kid's voice, he looked up.

Timothy stopped stock still and almost dropped his books. The man of the mist was standing there, the man who had said he was the spirit of the mountain. He was just standing there at the corner with Topcat on one arm and he was smiling at Timothy through his scraggly beard.

"Is this the right cat?" he asked gently.

Topcat stared at Timothy with his great golden eyes and stirred as if to come to him. The man handed the cat gently into Timothy's arms.

"Where did you find him? How did you get him?" Timothy asked, his heart thumping with relief against the warmth of the cat against him.

"I was coming down the mountain this morning—to see you," the man said. "And there he was."

"Walking along like he was king of the mountain?" Timothy asked.

"Exactly," the man said, "exactly like that. And I said to him, 'You are the king cat of this mountain and I am its spirit. I believe we had better go down and clear things up for our friend Timothy.'"

"Did you see all that stuff—the paper and all?"

"We mountain spirits stop in places for supplies," he winked. "Do you think your teacher might let me visit there at school?"

"We could declare you a qualified fourth grader," Timothy laughed. When Timothy and the bearded man walked through the playground together, the kids just stood back and stared.

That night at dinner, Mom served fried chicken and creamed gravy on mashed potatoes and sliced jellied cranberry sauce, the kind of food that Timothy liked the very best. Toby said, "What was this about the strange man actually coming down out of the mountain and telling every one it was his fault about your crazy story?"

Emily said, "Did the man really have a beard and come carrying your cat?"

So Timothy got to tell the whole story, right there at dinner. Everybody listened. He didn't add a single bit of stretch to it anywhere (except maybe how tall the man was or how long his beard was). He explained that it was his teacher, Mrs. Janson, who had decided to call the newspaper man and Mr. Hardesty came right over. He got an interview with pictures of the bearded man. "I was really trying to get the little kid to go home," the stranger told Mr. Hardesty. "Who would have thought he had enough spunk to go back up there in the mist looking for his cat?"

While Mr. Hardesty was there, he took more pictures of Topcat in his castle and in Timothy's arms. "I'll make you look older in these pictures if I have to touch them up," he reassured Timothy.

By that night everybody had read the bearded man's story in the paper. The phone kept ringing and people came in and out. Timothy was surprised and amazed by the way everyone acted.

Mrs. Nelson was the first. Mom and Dad exchanged a quick hopeless look as she came in, the folded paper in her hand.

She looked about quickly, her eyes mopping the corners as they always did. Then she took a chair and made a small "oof" as she sat down. Then she shook her head.

"Never have been able to figure boys," she said, "or men either," she added crossly, giving Dad an angled glance.

Mom and Dad just sat there on the edges of their chairs, waiting. Timothy noticed his mother twisting her apron a little in her lap and he felt very sorry.

"Never thought they'd care that much about a critter," she went on, frowning as if confused. "Or need a something to love that much."

Mom nodded as Mrs. Nelson went on.

"And that cat. It didn't seem all that dirty or mean a creature to see it like that on his shoulder." She thumped the paper with her hand.

"Awfully nice cat," Dad agreed, having to clear his throat.

"And I've been thinking about rodents, too," Mrs. Nelson went on fiercely. "I see the little holes around and the burrows that moles make under the privet. I lost a rapiolepsis last spring," she said angrily. "Pink Lady it was . . . moles!"

Timothy's mother clucked her tongue sympathetically. Timothy's father hid a grin. Timothy and his father both knew that Mom could never remember one plant's name from another. She wouldn't know a rapiolepsis from a zinnia if they both sat down across from her.

"So, in short, Timothy," she said, not even smiling, "there's more than a chance that all this newspaper fame will bring that cat's owners to claim him. But if it don't, when school is over and that cat needs a summer home, you might just put your hand up for it and say that Mrs. Nelson agreed. For the varmints, you see . . ."

She rose heavily from her chair. Timothy's mother and father exploded with "thank yous." Timothy went over all by himself without prompting.

"I just . . . just can't thank you enough," he said. "Gee, Mrs. Nelson."

She stared down at him, "You'd think some boys were just like people, wouldn't you?"

"You might think that," Dad agreed, seeing her to the door.

Even Toby acted different. When the house quieted down, she came in to where he was doing his homework. When she leaned over his shoulder, she smelled good. "How about I make a little basket for Topcat, Timmy?" she asked gently. "I could line it with gingham . . . or some Russian print if you'd like it better. Would he be happy in a basket after a castle of his own and all . . . with a moat, and a drawbridge?"

"He'd love it, Toby," Timothy told her. "And so would I."

"I'll listen to you more too, Timmy," she said gently.

Emily, being littler and the youngest and spoiled and all didn't want to give anything, but in her way she made Timothy happy too.

"Timmy," she asked wistfully, "when your Topcat comes, if I promise not to breathe, can I just pet him, outside or something where his hairs won't get on me?"

"Sure you can, Emmy," he told her. "Anyway, I'll brush him every day so that not that many hairs will fly around. But you'll have to stay out of my room . . . hear?"

"Oh, I do. I always do," she said innocently, her wide blue eyes full on his face.

"I could tell you a thing about telling fibs, Emmy," he said reproachingly.

"Look who's giving truth lessons!" Dad laughed, lowering his paper.

"I have the cure," Timothy said. "Forever and forever." He could see it now. Someday he would grow up and be awfully famous. Then he'd have another picture in some paper. And it would say, "Timothy Taylor, noted for his not ever fibbing, was given a huge award today for being famous."

"Dreams are all right as long as you know the difference," Dad laughed, just as if he could look right inside Timothy's head.